This Walker book belongs to:

_____

_____

First published 1999 by Walker Books Ltd
87 Vauxhall Walk, London SE11 5HJ

This edition published 2008

2 4 6 8 10 9 7 5 3 1

© 1999 Guy Parker-Rees

The moral rights of the author-illustrator have been asserted.

This book has been typeset in Cafeteria.

Printed in China

British Library Cataloguing in Publication Data: a catalogue
record for this book is available from the British Library.

ISBN 978-1-4063-1674-2

www.walkerbooks.co.uk

Little Jim Lost

Guy Parker-Rees

WALKER BOOKS
AND SUBSIDIARIES
LONDON · BOSTON · SYDNEY · AUCKLAND

Little Jim
lived in the
jungle ...

with his mum.

They played
and ate and
slept together,
in the
sunshine ...

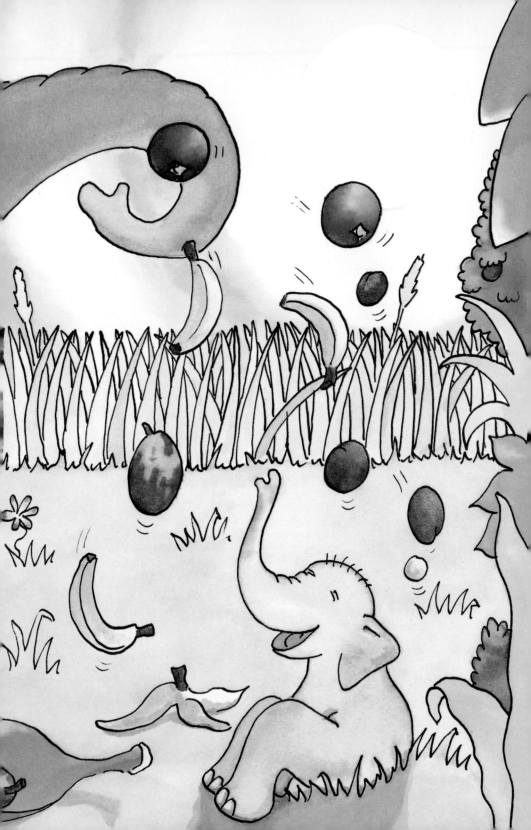

and the rain.

But one day
they were
playing hide-
and-seek ...

and Little Jim got lost.

He couldn't find his mum among the thick leaves ...

or in the
long grass.

He couldn't
find his mum
on the high
mountains ...

or in the deep river.

Little Jim felt very lonely. He climbed on to an island. But ...

it wasn't an island...

It was Little Jim's mum!
"I've been looking for
you everywhere!"
she said.

And she gave Little Jim
a big splashy hug!

WALKER BOOKS is the world's leading
independent publisher of children's books.
Working with the best authors and illustrators
we create books for all ages, from babies
to teenagers – books your child will
grow up with and always remember. So…

FOR THE BEST CHILDREN'S BOOKS,
LOOK FOR THE BEAR